Quentin Blake

Three Little Monkeys Ride Again

Illustrated By

Emma Chichester Clark

HarperCollins *Children's Books*

First published in hardback in Great Britain by HarperCollins *Children's Books* Ltd in 2019
First published in paperback in 2022

HarperCollins *Children's Books* is a division of HarperCollins*Publishers* Ltd
1 London Bridge Street, London SE1 9GF

www.harpercollins.co.uk

HarperCollins*Publishers*
1st Floor, Watermarque Building, Ringsend Road, Dublin 4, Ireland

1 3 5 7 9 10 8 6 4 2

Text copyright © Quentin Blake 2019
Illustrations copyright © Emma Chichester Clark 2019, 2022

ISBN: 978–0–00–824369–2

Printed in the UK by Pureprint

Some people take their dog on holiday.
Some people take their cat.

But Hilda Snibbs was taking her
three little monkeys. Their names
were Tim and Sam and Lulu. They
were going to visit Hilda's mother.

"Two or three days of peace and
quiet in the country," she said,
"will do us no end of good."

Hilda's mother lived in a little house beside a river.

There were tall trees, and the river was full of ducks and frogs and pondweed.

It was very calm and peaceful.

"We must go out and do some shopping for lunch," said Hilda's mother. "We can unpack your suitcase when we come back."

"We shan't be gone long," said Hilda to Tim and Sam and Lulu.
"You must be very good while we're away."

But the three little monkeys very soon began to feel bored.

They went up to the bedroom.
They unpacked Hilda's suitcase.

They unpacked the
chest of drawers.

They unpacked an old chest full of
crockery they found under the bed.

When Hilda and her mother came back – **what a sight!**

Hilda's mother nearly fainted.

Hilda said, "You naughty monkeys. Why on earth did I bring you on holiday?"

Tim and Sam and Lulu looked at her
with their big round eyes and said nothing.

The next morning Hilda and her mother went out to buy some tea and biscuits.

"We shan't be gone long," said Hilda to Tim and Sam and Lulu. "You must be very good while we're away."

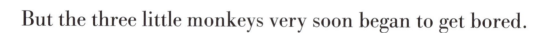
But the three little monkeys very soon began to get bored.

They went into the hall
and took all the hats
into the garden.

And the wellington boots.
And the umbrellas.
And the shopping trolley.

And Hilda's mother's favourite portrait
of her grandfather.

When Hilda and her mother came back –
what a sight!

Hilda's mother nearly fainted.

"You naughty little monkeys," said Hilda.
"This is the **last time** I bring you
on holiday."

Tim and Sam and Lulu looked at her
with their big round eyes and said nothing.

Later on Hilda and her mother thought they would go for a calming stroll in the evening air.

"We shan't be gone long," said Hilda to Tim and Sam and Lulu. "You must be **very** good while we're away."

But the three little monkeys soon began to feel bored.

They went into the potting shed
and got out the wheelbarrow.

And the watering cans.

And the garden tools.

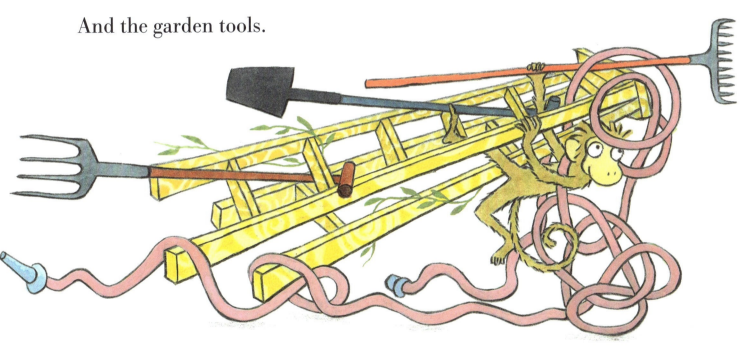

And the stepladder.

And twenty-seven empty flowerpots,
and a large ball of garden string.

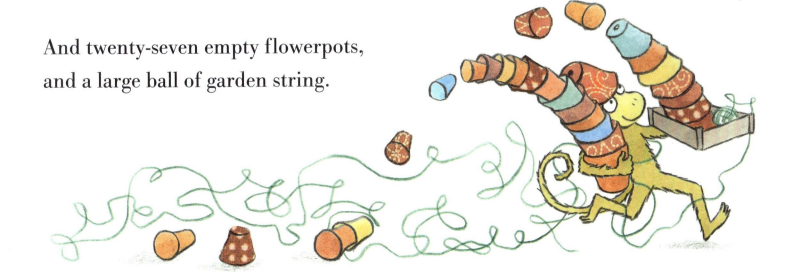

When Hilda and her mother came back –
what a sight!

Hilda's mother nearly fainted.

"You naughty little monkeys," said Hilda.
"I shall **never, never** take you
on holiday again."

Tim and Sam and Lulu looked at her
with their big round eyes
and said nothing.

The next morning Hilda went out to buy her mother
a box of chocolates as a present.

It was a sunny day and her mother
    was going to sit in the garden and rest.

"I shan't be gone long,"
Hilda said to Tim and Sam
and Lulu.

"You must be **very good**
while I'm away."

Hilda's mother dozed off in her chair, and
the little monkeys soon began to feel bored.

So . . . they got all the laundry from
the washing line,

vests, blouses,

knickers, tea towels,

aprons and nightshirts

and three tablecloths from the kitchen,
and an old raincoat,

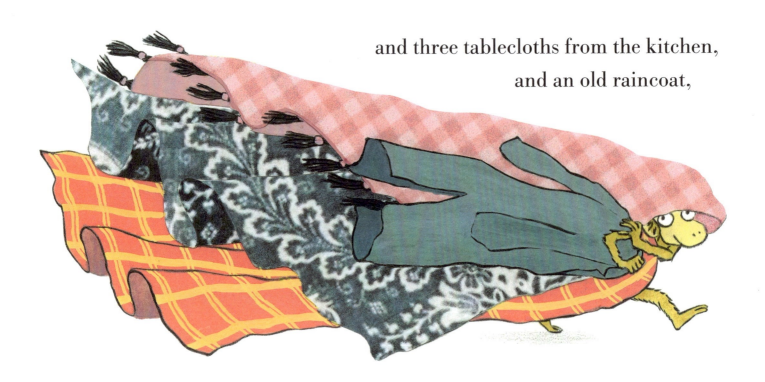

and started to cover up
Hilda's mother with it.

And then they got the tarpaulin
from the log pile beside the house,

and put it

right

over

the top.

At that moment there was a rumble
of thunder and the sky turned black . . .

And it rained … and it rained … and it rained.

When Hilda came back the rain had stopped.

But what had become of her mother?

She wasn't in
the potting shed.

She wasn't under the trees.

But what was that where her
mother's chair used to be?

She pulled off the tarpaulin
and the tablecloths
and the raincoat
and there was all the laundry,
perfectly dry and safe and sound,
and so was her mother.

"You **wonderful** little monkeys," said Hilda.
"**Thank goodness** I brought you on holiday."

Tim and Sam and Lulu looked at her
with their big round eyes and said nothing.

And then they all went into the kitchen to make a cup of tea.

There were ducks in the sink and in the saucepans, and there were frogs in the soup and in the rice pudding,

and there was pondweed
everywhere.

But that is the sort of thing you have to expect
if you take three little monkeys on holiday.